THE·LAND·OF
NOD

THE
BLACK
MOUNTAIN

THE
FLOATING
ISLES

SNOWY
VILLAGE

ENCHANTED
VALLEY

CREEPY
CASTLE

GLOOMY
DEN

GLITTER
BAY

BOULDER
GORGE

N

W E

S

For Jane and Emma,
my Christmas pixies
R.F.

For Jessica
C.C.

LADYBIRD BOOKS

UK | USA | Canada | Ireland | Australia | India | New Zealand | South Africa
Ladybird Books is part of the Penguin Random House group of companies
whose addresses can be found at global.penguinrandomhouse.com.
www.penguin.co.uk   www.puffin.co.uk   www.ladybird.co.uk

Penguin
Random House
UK

First published 2019
001
Written by Rhiannon Fielding. Text copyright © Ladybird Books Ltd, 2019
Illustrations copyright © Chris Chatterton, 2019
Moral rights asserted
Printed in China
A CIP catalogue record for this book is available from the British Library
ISBN: 978–0–241–41457–6
All correspondence to:
Ladybird Books, Penguin Random House Children's
80 Strand, London WC2R 0RL

MIX
Paper from
responsible sources
FSC® C018179

TEN MINUTES TO BED

Little Unicorn's Christmas

Rhiannon Fielding • Chris Chatterton

One cold winter evening that glittered so bright,
in a forest that sparkled with magical light,
Twinkle the unicorn pranced through the trees . . .

for that very night it would be
Christmas Eve.

The setting sun turned to a **golden-pink glow,**
but Twinkle was still rolling round in the snow.

"Ten minutes to bed!"
called her dad with a sigh . . .

but something above her
had caught Twinkle's eye.

It couldn't be Father Christmas's sleigh . . .
bedtime was still nine minutes away!
But with jingling bells, and a crash and a sneeze,
something huge landed
among the tall trees.

Into the glade came a man dressed in red,
with a fluffy white beard, and a hat on his head.
"Eight minutes to bed!" said the man with a shiver.

"And hundreds
of presents still
left to deliver!"

"One of my **reindeer** – can you guess who? –
is tucked up at home as he's got reindeer flu.

Seven minutes to bed
– it's a bit of a blow –

we've still got twenty-two
countries to go!"

He whistled and, suddenly, standing right there
was a sleigh and eight reindeer, all snorting the air.
Father Christmas was here – it was real! It was true!

With six minutes to bed
Twinkle knew what to do.

There was Dasher and Dancer, then Prancer and Vixen,
Comet and Cupid, then Donner and Blitzen . . .
with Twinkle the unicorn
leading the way!

"Five minutes!" called Dad.

"Good luck, little sleigh."

Soaring along, then swooping down low,

over oceans and mountains all covered in snow,

with **four minutes to bed,** the sleigh travelled fast,

powered by **unicorn glitter** at last!

Each time they stopped, with **clattering hooves,**
and landed on boulders, or islands, or roofs,

Santa dropped off the presents
then called out the time:

"Three minutes to go, team!
Up! Time to shine!"

As they drew close to the last of the stops,

Twinkle caught sight of some leafy treetops.

"Two minutes to bed," Santa said with a wink . . .

"We couldn't have done it
without you, young Twink."

From his sack he pulled out a **small gift** wrapped in red;

he gave it to Twinkle, then patted her head.

"One minute to bedtime – that goes for us, too!"

And with one final jingle,
away the sleigh flew.

Tucked up in bed, as she closed her tired eyes,

Twinkle pictured great oceans, and rivers, and skies.

And soon she was sleeping and deep in her dreams,

on the soft leafy ground,
under silver moonbeams.

THE·LAND·OF
NOD

THE
BLACK
MOUNTAIN

THE
FLOATING
ISLES

SNOWY
VILLAGE

ENCHANTED
VALLEY

CREEPY
CASTLE

GLOOMY
DEN

BOULDER
GORGE

GLITTER
BAY

N
W   E
S

THE
ANCIENT FOREST

OUTER
SPACE

EMERALD
GLEN

DEADLY
CREEK

GIANTS' TOWN

THE
STINKY
SWAMPS

GOLDEN
COVE

RICKETY
BRIDGE

Look out for more bedtime adventures in

THE·LAND·OF NOD

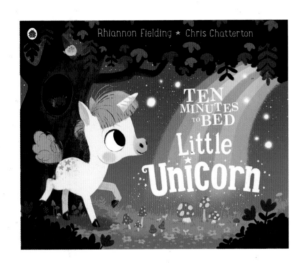